What Was He Doing, Anyway?

What would his father say? Risking his life to save a dragon? An enemy of his people? A dragon that *he* might even have to face one day on his own dragon-quest? He could still turn back. It was not too late. Perhaps he should just let the creature be found and killed.

Darek walked slowly out to the barn. The soft hiccuping sound still came from inside. He opened the door and the dragonling rushed out and rubbed happily against him.

"Thrrummm, thrrummm, thrrummm," it said.

Darek stroked its scaly head. "Why did you have to come here?" he whispered. Then he looked over at the lifeless body of the Great Blue. "I guess it wasn't your idea either, was it? Come, then. I'll take you home, but after that I never want to see you again, understand?"

The Dragonling

Jackie French Koller

Illustrated by Judith Mitchell

A MINSTREL® BOOK

Published by POCKET BOOKS
New York   London   Toronto   Sydney   Tokyo   Singapore

To Devin,
because dragons are his second favorite animals,
next to dogs

A Minstrel Book published by
POCKET BOOKS, a division of Simon & Schuster Inc.
1230 Avenue of the Americas, New York, NY 10020

Text copyright © 1990 by Jackie Lynn Koller
Illustrations copyright © 1990 by Judith Mitchell

Published by arrangement with Little, Brown and Company (Inc.)

ISBN: 0-671-86790-3

First Minstrel Books printing December 1995

10 9 8 7 6 5 4 3 2

A MINSTREL BOOK and colophon are registered trademarks of Simon & Schuster Inc.

Cover art by Judith Mitchell

Printed in the U.S.A.

1

Darek awoke at the first light of dawn. He sat up quickly and pushed his bed curtains aside. Through his window he could see the soft, violet rays of the morning sun just touching the tips of the yellow mountains of Orr. His brother, Clep, was up there somewhere, probably breaking camp, getting ready for the day's hunt. It wasn't fair, Darek thought. Why did he have to wait three more years before *his* first dragonquest? So what if Clep was twelve and he was only nine. He was nearly as tall and strong as Clep. Three more years! It seemed like forever.

"Darek? Darek, are you up?" It was his mother's voice from the kitchen below.

"I'm coming," Darek called back. He got dressed and clattered down the stairs.

His mother was bent over the hearth, spooning porridge into his bowl. Darek slid into his place at the table.

"Do you think maybe the men will be home today?" he asked.

His mother's brow wrinkled with worry as she served him his breakfast.

"Who knows how long they will be gone?" she said. "Ten days? Twenty? A dragonquest ends when it ends."

"I can't wait until it's my turn," Darek said eagerly. "I will be the one to make the kill. I will win the claws to wear around my neck. I will be the Marksman, like Father."

Darek's mother shook her head and turned back to the fire.

2

"Why are you silent, Mother?" Darek asked. "Why don't you get excited about the dragonquest like everyone else?"

"My brother was killed on his dragonquest," said Darek's mother quietly.

"Many have been killed on the dragonquests," said Darek, "but they are heroes. You should be proud."

Darek's mother sighed. "In the old days," she said, "when the dragons were plentiful, when they threatened the villages and raided the yuke* herds, that was the time for heroes. Now the dragons are few, and they keep to the mountains. Why should we send young boys into their midst?"

"They are not boys," said Darek. "They are men, and they must face a dragon to prove it."

"There are other ways to prove you are a man," said Darek's mother.

*yuke: a white, long-haired animal, much like a goat, only larger.

"What are they then?" asked Darek.

"Doing your work with pride, caring for others, and thinking your own thoughts are good ways," said Darek's mother.

"*Bah,*" said Darek. "Anyone can do those things, but only a man can slay a dragon."

There was a sudden, loud clanging and Darek's mother's head jerked up.

"The men return," she said.

Darek and his mother ran to the village square. The hunting party was threading its way down through the mountain pass, pulling a great wagon. Upon it lay a hulking mound.

"A Blue!" shouted Darek. "It's a Great Blue!" Great Blues were the largest and fiercest of all dragons. Darek could hardly contain his excitement as he raced to meet the party. But as he drew closer, his steps faltered. He could see that his father was leading a yuke, and slung over the yuke's saddle was a small

body, about the size of Clep's. Darek heard his mother cry out behind him.

Other children jostled Darek as they rushed by. "What's the matter? Hurry up! Get out of the way!" Darek swallowed hard and tried to ignore the great weight that had settled in his chest. If it *was* Clep he must be brave. He must not shed a tear. He must be honored to have a hero for a brother.

Then a voice called out. "Darek! Mother! Over here!" A yuke broke out of the hunting party, and Darek saw that its rider was Clep. Relief rushed over him as he ran to meet his brother.

Clep swung himself down out of the saddle. He held up a necklace. A necklace made of claws! "I made the kill!" he shouted. "I killed a Great Blue!"

Darek fought back a pang of jealousy. "I can't believe it!" he shouted, thumping Clep on the back. "You? The Marksman!"

Darek's mother came up beside them.

There was joy and relief in her eyes as she hugged Clep tightly to her, but when he held up the bloodstained necklace, she looked away.

"Who is the fallen one?" she asked quietly.

Clep's face grew grave. "It is Yoran," he said.

The weight came back to Darek's chest. Yoran? Clep's best friend? Yoran, who had been like a second brother in their house ever since Darek could remember? Yoran, who ran faster than the wind? How could it be he who lay so still now across the saddle?

Darek's mother nodded, her face like stone. "I must go to his mother," she said.

2

Darek couldn't sleep. He was too excited about the festival tomorrow. His brother, Clep, and all of their family would be the guests of honor. There would be dancing and feasting, and then at night, a great bonfire in which the body of the dragon would be burned. Now it lay on the wagon, just outside the paddock fence. Tomorrow night its ashes would be placed in a carved urn and given to Clep. Clep would place the urn on the mantel, next to his father's. One day Darek vowed to place an urn there too.

Outside, in the paddock, Darek could hear the nervous rustling of the yukes. It made them uneasy to have the body of the dragon so near. Darek listened. The house was still. No one would know if he went down to comfort Nonni, his favorite, and gave her a bit of sugar. He crept out in his nightshirt.

"Here, Nonni, little pet," he whispered. The small yuke ran to his side and nuzzled him gently. Darek took the sugar from his pocket and fed it to her. Her rough, wet tongue tickled his hand as she licked every crumb from between his fingers.

Darek stared at the great dragon. He could see it clearly in the light of Zoriak's twin moons. It lay on its side, its wings twisted and crumpled, its once fearsome claws stubby and blunt. Darek got goose bumps thinking about how it must have looked in life. He walked around it, imagining it standing on its powerful legs, flames shooting from its mouth. He could see it charge. He could hear it roar. He could hear it . . . whimper?

Darek jumped back. He was sure he had heard something. Could the creature still be alive? Darek wasn't taking any chances. He dived for cover behind a barliberry bush and lay still, waiting. The sound came again, *huf-uh huf-uh,* a soft hiccuping kind of sob. Darek peeked out. The great head lay just in front of him, still as death. He crept out of hiding and circled the creature once again. Then he saw it — a tiny head peeking out of the pouch on the giant dragon's belly. *A dragonling!*

Darek stared in amazement. He knew dragons carried their young in pouches until they were old enough to fend for themselves, but he had never seen a live dragonling before. The small creature came out of the pouch and climbed unsteadily up its mother's chest. It was about half as big as Darek, and he guessed it to be very young, maybe even new-born.

The dragonling licked its mother's still face with its forked tongue, whimpering all the while. Darek stepped back and slipped on a pebble, falling to the ground. The dragonling twisted its neck and looked at him, its eyes shining pale green in the night.

"*Rrronk,*" it said and began to climb down in his direction.

Darek scrambled to his feet. Small as the creature was, it was still a dragon, and Darek had no wish to face it unarmed. He picked up a big stick. The dragonling fluttered down off the wagon and approached on wobbly legs.

"*Rrronk,*" it said again.

Darek held the stick out like a sword. The dragonling stopped and sniffed it. It gave it a lick, then whimpered again. Darek had been taught all his life to hate and fear dragons, but it was hard to hate such a small one, and

an orphan at that. He lowered his club, and the dragonling came up and nuzzled him.

Darek felt in his pocket. There was a small lump of sugar left. He held it out cautiously. The little dragon sniffed it, then the forked tongue flicked out, and it was gone.

"*Thrrrummmm,*" said the dragon. It was a happy sound. The dragon nuzzled him again.

"I don't have any more," said Darek, holding both hands up. "See?"

The dragon butted him playfully.

"All right, all right," said Darek. "I'll get more. Wait here." He turned and started toward the house. The dragon wobbled after him.

"No," said Darek, quickening his steps. "You stay."

"*Rrronk,*" said the dragon. It flapped its small wings and flew a few feet to catch up.

Darek stopped and stared at it, suddenly realizing what he'd done. He'd made friends with a dragon, an enemy of his people. Now what was he supposed to do?

3

Darek struggled to close the barn door, pushing the dragonling back in.

"You've got to wait here," he said. "And don't make a sound."

"*Rrronk,*" said the dragon.

"You don't understand," said Darek. "They'll kill you if they find you." He gave a final push, then pulled the door tight and lowered the latch. He could hear the orphan's muffled whimpers on the other side. He had to hurry or someone else might wake and hear.

Darek crept up to his room, dressed quickly, then tiptoed down to the back room where the weapons were kept. He slung his bow over his shoulder and strapped his quiver of arrows in place. On his way through the kitchen he filled a sack with supplies. It would be a journey of many days.

Suddenly he stopped and wondered. What do dragonlings eat? Perhaps such a young one would still need milk. He would have to bring along a female yuke. Dorlass, whose calf had been born dead, had milk to spare, but she would not nurse a dragonling. Darek packed a waterskin so he could feed the creature by hand.

Darek paused in the kitchen doorway and looked back. His stomach twisted into a knot. What was he doing, anyway? What would his father say? Risking his life to save a dragon? An enemy of his people? A dragon that *he* might even have to face one day on his own dragonquest? He could still turn back. It was not too late. Perhaps he should just let the creature be found and killed. After all, what more did a dragon deserve?

Darek walked slowly out to the barn. The soft, hiccuping sound still came from inside. He opened the door and the dragonling rushed out and rubbed happily against him.

"*Thrrummm, thrrummmm, thrrummmm,*" it said.

Darek stroked its scaly head. "Why did you have to come here?" he whispered. Then he looked over at the lifeless body of the Great Blue. "I guess it wasn't your idea either, was it? Come then. I'll take you home, but after that I never want to see you again, understand?"

The dragonling thrummed happily. Darek took out another lump of sugar and let the orphan lick it from his hand. The sky was slowly growing lighter.

"Come on," said Darek, "we've got to go."

He led Dorlass out of the paddock. She was

skittish around the dragonling. It kept running in and out between her legs, making her buck and jump while Darek was trying to get her saddle pack strapped on.

"Cut that out," said Darek, giving the dragonling a gentle kick.

"*Rrronk, rrronk, rrronk,*" it screeched, then it half ran, half flew back up to its mother's body and dove into her pouch.

Darek finished securing the saddle, then he led Dorlass over to the Great Blue. "Hey," he whispered, "come on out of there."

He saw a lump wiggle around in the pouch, but the dragonling did not appear.

"Come on, don't be such a baby," Darek coaxed. "I hardly even touched you."

The dragonling poked its head out. "*Rrronk,*" it said.

"I'm sorry," said Darek. "I thought dragons were tough."

He held out another piece of sugar, and the dragon crept slowly down again. Darek fed

17

it and scratched its head until it was thrumming happily. "Some fighter you're going to make," he whispered.

Darek led Dorlass out to the road. The dragonling followed.

"You're going to have to move faster than that," said Darek, "if we're going to get to the pass before sunrise." He ran forward a few steps and then called to the dragonling. It flapped its wings and flew to catch up. Running and calling, running and calling, Darek managed to get to the foothills just as the first rays of the sun peeked over the mountaintops. Suddenly the little dragon turned back.

"Where are you going?" yelled Darek. He ran after the dragonling and grabbed it gently by the wings. It struggled to get away.

"*Rrronk,*" it squawked, "*rrronk!*"

It was staring back down the hill at the body of its mother.

Darek stroked its head.

"I know," he said. "It is *rrronk.*"

4

_____

"I guess if we're going to be together awhile I ought to give you a name," said Darek. "Are you a boy or a girl?"

The little creature didn't answer. It had spied an insect of some kind on the path, and it was all bent over, nose to the ground. Suddenly the insect bit it.

"_Rrronk, rrronk,_" it screeched, running over and shoving its head up under Darek's shirt.

"Will you get out of here!" yelled Darek, giving the creature a push and pulling his shirt back down. "I'm not your mother and I don't have a pouch."

The dragonling lay down and curled itself around his legs.

"You're the sorriest excuse for a dragon I've ever seen," Darek said, peeling the orphan off his legs. Then he noticed its belly.

"You don't have a pouch either," he said. "That means you must be a boy."

"*Huf-uh, huf-uh,*" the dragonling sobbed, rubbing its nose with its forefoot.

"It's only a bug bite, for pity's sake," said Darek. "You have to toughen up. I'll give you a strong name, a powerful name. Then maybe you'll try a little harder to live up to it. I will call you Zantor, King of the Dragons."

Zantor whimpered and pushed his head under Darek's arm. "Well," Darek said, "maybe you'll grow into it."

By evening Zantor was moving very slowly and stumbling often.

"It's been a long day for you, hasn't it?"

said Darek. "We'll stop now and camp for the night."

Zantor moaned softly and nuzzled Darek's pocket.

"The sugar is all gone," said Darek. "But I'll get you some milk."

He set to work milking Dorlass, and when he had filled the waterskin, he held it up over the dragonling's head. "Drink," he said, letting loose a stream.

The milk squirted in Zantor's eyes and dripped off his nose, but he made no attempt to drink it.

"Didn't your mother teach you anything?" said Darek. He opened the dragon's mouth with one hand and squirted the milk in with the other. Zantor started to sputter and choke. Darek stopped squirting, and the little dragon shook his head and spit all the milk back out.

"Look," said Darek, "it may not be your mother's, but it's all we have."

Zantor clamped his mouth shut and refused to drink.

Darek shrugged. Maybe dragons *didn't* nurse their babies. Maybe baby dragons ate regular food right away. It was worth a try. "I'll be right back," he said, shouldering his bow. "You wait here."

Darek didn't know whether Zantor understood or whether he was just too tired to move, but whatever the reason, he obeyed.

There were plenty of animals in the mountain forest, and Darek was a good shot. He quickly brought down a small glibbet* and carried it back to Zantor.

"There," he said, laying the animal at the dragon's feet. "Now eat." Darek sat down and laid out his own supper, some bread and cheese and a big cluster of barliberries.

Zantor sniffed at the glibbet, then he whimpered and began digging a hole. The next thing Darek knew, the dragonling had buried it.

*glibbet: a small, weasel-like animal

"Hey," said Darek, "what are you doing? You can't save that. You have to eat it now. We're moving on in the morning."

Darek dug the glibbet up again, but when he turned around he found Zantor happily munching on *his* barliberries.

"Well I'll be," said Darek. "You eat barliberries? What else do you eat?" He went into the woods and gathered all the herbs and nuts and berries he could find. Zantor gulped them greedily and followed him back to find more. At last they were both full, and Darek set about building a campfire. He gathered sticks and dry leaves, then he took out his flint and struck it against a rock. A spark flew out and landed on the leaves. Darek blew on it. It flared a moment, then died. Darek tried again. This time Zantor bent down, right next to him, staring intently. Darek blew on the spark. It sputtered and went out.

"Drat," said Darek. Then suddenly, *Whoosh!* A stream of flame shot by his nose.

Darek jumped back. It was Zantor! Zantor was breathing fire!

In no time at all the campfire was burning merrily. Zantor sat back on his hind legs, looking quite proud.

"Wow," said Darek. "That was pretty good. I didn't know you could do that yet."

Zantor thrummed happily, then curled up next to the campfire and went to sleep.

Darek stared at him. "You really are the strangest dragon I've ever heard of," he whispered, then he rolled his blanket out on the other side of the campfire and lay down.

The night was dark and damp, and the woods were full of strange calls and rustlings. Darek began to wish he were home in his own warm bed. He missed his family. Perhaps the little dragon felt lonely too, because before long Darek heard a soft scuffling, and then a small body nestled up against his own.

5

Darek awoke to find Zantor still snuggled up beside him.

"Sleep well?" he asked.

The dragon thrummed and licked him on the cheek.

"Will you cut that out?" said Darek. "You're supposed to be tough, remember?"

Darek made himself a breakfast of bread and barliberry jam while Zantor foraged in the woods, obviously remembering all the places Darek had shown him the night before.

"Pretty smart, aren't you?" said Darek when the dragon came back. Zantor looked healthier already. His scales, which had been dull and greenish, were now turning a shiny, peacock blue.

That day and the next two passed much like the first, except that Zantor grew stronger each day and was able to move more quickly. By the fourth day they were getting close to the Valley of the Dragons. Darek had never been there, but he had heard it described so many times around the campfire that he knew just what to look for.

"Won't be long now," he told Zantor. "You'll be home by afternoon." Zantor thrummed happily, and Darek wondered again if he somehow understood. Darek suddenly grew sad at the thought of leaving the dragonling behind. "That's what you came here for," he scolded himself angrily. "He's only a dragon, after all." But still, Darek worried. What would the other dragons think of

Zantor, with his strange and gentle ways? Would they accept him, or treat him as an outcast? Or worse, would they kill him?

Darek and Zantor came upon the twin stones that marked the entrance to the valley, and Darek realized that they must proceed carefully. He tied Dorlass to a tree, then crept up to the top of a ridge to look out over the valley. Zantor scrambled up beside him.

"Get down, stupid," said Darek, throwing an arm around Zantor's neck and pulling him down.

"*Rrronk, rrronk,*" said Zantor, struggling to get free.

"*Shhhush!*" said Darek. Then he pointed down into the valley. "Look!"

Darek's heart pounded. For all his brave talk, he was unprepared for the size and number of creatures moving about below. Some of them lazed in the sun. Others waded in the river. Smaller ones butted heads together and tumbled like children in the dirt. There were caves cut into the mountains all around the valley, and occasionally a dragon would appear at the mouth of one and glide down on great wings to the valley floor. They were mostly Yellow Crested dragons, with a few Green Horned. Darek saw no Great Blues at all.

Zantor was staring at the scene excitedly.

"Is this your home?" Darek asked him. "Where are your kind?"

Zantor turned his head and looked toward the mountain on the right, high up at the very largest caves. There was a sudden movement in the shadows, and then a Great Blue stepped full into the sun. She stood poised for a moment on the edge, then lifted off and soared out almost over their heads.

"*Thrummmm, thrummmm, thrummmm,*" said Zantor.

"*Shhush!*" whispered Darek, clamping a hand over the dragonling's mouth. Darek stared up in awe at the Great Blue. She was the most magnificent creature he had ever seen. The sun glinted on her deep blue scales, making them sparkle like the sea. Her wings stretched out silver and shimmering against the pale blue sky. For all her great size, she was sleek in the air, and when she landed gracefully on the valley floor she stood head and shoulders above the rest, like a queen.

Darek let go of Zantor's mouth. Zantor thrummed again, happily staring down at the Great Blue. Darek smiled and nodded.

"Yes," he said. "I think she would make you a fine mother."

6

Getting the Great Blue to adopt Zantor would be tricky. Zantor was not yet strong enough to fly down into the valley himself, and Darek wasn't about to *walk* him down. The best chance, he decided, would be to get the dragonling up to the Great Blue's cave while she was away. If she came home and found him in her nest, she might be more likely to accept him as her own.

Knowing what to do, and doing it, however, were two different matters. The cave was high up on the mountainside. Climbing would be difficult, and worse, they would be in plain sight of the dragons. Darek decided that they'd make the climb at night, and then hide in the bushes near the mouth of the cave until the Great Blue went out in the morning.

Darek ate a large supper of cheese and milk and bread, and then topped it off with a generous helping of berries that he and Zantor found. When the sun went down, Zantor started scuffling around, nose to the ground. He pushed a couple of sticks together and started to blow on them.

"No, Zantor," said Darek. "No campfire tonight." He picked up the sticks and tossed them into the woods. Far back down the mountain pass, a bright flicker in the darkness caught his eye.

A campfire. Darek took a deep breath and let it out slowly. It was a search party, he was sure. His father and Clep and the others had come after him. He'd been so busy thinking ahead that he'd never thought back about the trail he was leaving. He guessed them to be about a day's journey behind him. He still had a chance to make his plan work, but there would be no second chances.

Darek sat down and looked at Zantor.

"I don't know if you understand me at all," he said, "but what I have to say is very important. You and I are going up there." He pointed to himself, then to Zantor, then to the cave. "We're going now. Tonight. Do you understand?"

Zantor stared where Darek pointed. "*Rrronk,*" he said.

"It *is* going to be *rrronk,*" said Darek, "but we can make it. Just follow me, and be *quiet.*" Darek put his hand around Zantor's mouth and held it shut to show him what quiet meant, then he moved off into the darkness. The dragonling followed.

Climbing was hard and slow. Zantor seemed better at it than Darek. He was lighter, for one thing, and his claws were good at finding niches to hold on to. Darek's hands grew sore and numb from the night chill. Several times he found himself wondering again why he was risking his life for a dragon.

Suddenly there was a piercing shriek. From a cave across the valley two dragons appeared. They roared and charged at each other. Their fiery breath lit up the night. Darek flattened himself against the rock, hoping the noise wouldn't awaken the Great Blue. Zantor whimpered. The two dragons, both Yellows, went on screeching for a while, then quieted down and went back into the same cave. Darek chuckled. "Perhaps they are husband and wife," he whispered to Zantor. "I've heard arguments like that back in the village."

Darek and Zantor edged onward. They had almost reached the cave when Darek felt himself slipping. He grabbed hold of a small bush and kicked out, madly trying to find safe footing. There was none. Darek's heart sank. His hands were so sore and tired he could hardly hang on. So this was how it was going to end? His father and Clep would find him dead at the bottom of the cliffs. What a fool he'd been.

Suddenly something tugged at the back of his neck and Darek felt himself rising. He was dragged up and up until he was on firm ground again. Zantor landed beside him, breathing heavily.

"You?" said Darek. "You lifted me up, with those little wings?" Zantor seemed too tired to answer. He just laid his head in Darek's lap. Darek stroked it gently.

"Maybe you *are* growing into your name," he whispered.

7

Darek and Zantor spent the rest of the night in the bushes outside the Great Blue's cave. At the stroke of dawn, before it was even fully light, the Great Blue appeared. The whole valley quickly came to life. With great squawks and chatterings, dragons appeared at the mouth of every cave and crisscrossed down through the air. The Great Blue lifted off.

Darek sucked in his breath. "Well," he said, "I guess this is it." He edged his way out of the bushes and into the cave, motioning to Zantor to follow. The cave was pitch-black inside, and Darek couldn't see a thing, but instantly the air was filled with a chorus of *rrronks*. Dragonlings! Zantor rushed past Darek back into the gloom, and the *rrronks* turned to excited thrummings.

Darek's eyes gradually adjusted to the darkness and at last he could make out Zantor and two other slightly larger dragonlings tumbling merrily over one another. Darek smiled. He wished he could give Zantor a farewell hug, but he knew the smartest thing to do was to leave, fast. Just as he turned to go, a huge shadow darkened the mouth of the cave.

"*Grrrawk! Grrrawk!*" shrieked the Great Blue as she touched down on the outer ledge. Darek's blood turned to ice. She must have heard her babies cry and come back to check on them. If only he'd waited until she was out of earshot! Her great bulk filled the entrance. Darek whirled, looking for another passageway. There was none. These were not ordinary caves, he realized, just holes in the mountains hollowed out by the dragons' sharp claws.

"*Grrrawk! Grrrawk!*" the dragon screeched again. She glared at him, her green eyes glowing in the dark. Darek swung his bow off his shoulder and reached back for an arrow. With a trembling hand he fitted it to the string. There was only one unprotected spot, he knew, high up on the neck, just under the chin. She would lift her head just before battle. He would have one chance.

The dragon reared back. Flames shot from her mouth and lit up the cave. Darek took aim and —

Whomp! Darek took a hard blow to the back. He fell forward, the wind knocked out of him. He twisted in the dirt, gulping and sucking for air. When at last he could breathe again, he rolled over. Zantor stood behind him.

"Traitor!" Darek hissed, knowing even as he said it how foolish it sounded. Wouldn't he have done the same thing in Zantor's place? The Great Blue reared back and roared again, and Darek put his head down and waited for the end.

But instead of flames, or teeth, or claws, he felt only a small pressure. Zantor had lain down on top of him.

The Great Blue stopped roaring and started pacing back and forth, as if trying to decide how to deal with this strange turn of events. Her own dragonlings came over to her and made small mewing sounds. She picked them up and dropped them gently into her pouch. Then she came over and touched noses with Zantor. He whimpered and made little mewing noises too. She licked him tenderly and he began to thrumm. She picked him up and put him into her pouch as well.

Darek was glad, at least, that the dragon had accepted Zantor. Now it was *his* turn.

With one claw the dragon ripped off Darek's quiver and tossed it over near his bow. In a mighty burst of flame the weapons disappeared. Darek cringed. With the same claw the dragon rolled him over. She sniffed him up and down and stared a long time into his eyes, then, to Darek's amazement, she hooked her claw through his shirt, picked him up, and dropped him into her pouch with the others.

Zantor nestled up against him. "*Thrrumm, thrrumm, thrrumm,*" he said. Darek let out a sigh of relief.

"I don't know what you told her," he said, "but thanks."

Darek was glad to be alive, but not at all sure what to expect next. He poked his head up. The Great Blue had turned and shuffled back out to the edge of the rock ledge. She plucked one of her dragonlings from the pouch and set him down before her.

"*Grok,*" she said. The dragonling wobbled

for a moment on the edge, then fluttered out into the air. The dragon lifted out the second dragonling.

"Oh, no." Darek groaned. "We *would* arrive just in time for flying lessons."

After the second dragonling was airborne, the Great Blue lifted out Zantor. Zantor stood timidly on the edge, his wings sagging. "*Rrronk?*" he said.

The mother dragon nudged him gently but firmly, and off he went. Darek closed his eyes, then opened one. Zantor flapped and fluttered for a moment, then straightened out and glided beautifully.

The next thing he knew, Darek found *himself* standing on the ledge. The drop to the valley below made his head swim and his knees feel like jelly. The Great Blue bent close and eyed him up and down. Then she turned him around and eyed him up and down again. Finally she snorted, picked him up, and put him back in her pouch.

The Great Blue lifted off and soared out over the valley. The wind whipped through Darek's hair and took his breath away. The ground raced by below him. He was flying! Suddenly Darek didn't even care if the dragons killed him in the end. The thrill of this moment made it all worthwhile.

The dragon made a surprisingly gentle landing. Zantor came running over, thrumming loudly, and jumped into the pouch with Darek. "Shush," said Darek, ducking down as far as he could. He was not sure the other dragons would accept him as readily as the Great Blue had.

All of the dragons had moved into the forest — hunting, Darek imagined. The Great Blue and her two dragonlings followed. Darek peeked out. To his amazement, the dragons were not hunting at all. They were feeding on fruits and nuts and leaves, just like Zantor.

8

Darek lay back with his head resting on Zantor's round belly. The Great Blue and the dragonlings were sleeping. All of the dragons, it seemed, returned to their caves for naps at midday. Darek was drowsy too, after his long night, but he was too excited to sleep. His mind was running in leaps and bounds. If the Zorians could befriend these dragons as he had, what a great help they could be to one another. Darek had noticed that food was not plentiful in the valley. Maybe that was why there were so few dragons left. The Zorians were great farmers. They could grow food for the dragons, and in return the dragons could help the Zorians in many ways. They could light fires. They could help plow the fields with their great claws. And *then,* there was the flying! Even a small dragon could probably carry four Zorians in its pouch at once. Journeys of several days could be made in hours! Darek could hardly wait to tell everyone of his discovery. He would probably become famous, maybe even go down in history. . . .

Darek finally fell asleep, dreaming of a bright new future for dragons and Zorians alike.

*   *   *

"*Grrrawk!*" Darek woke with a start. The Great Blue had jumped up and rushed, roaring, to the mouth of the cave. Darek scrambled to his feet. He edged along the side of the cave and peeked out. There on a ledge just below the cave were his father, Clep, and the full Zorian hunting party.

The Great Blue roared again, head up, flames shooting out. Dragons began to emerge from the other caves. The Zorians formed a battle circle, shields and weapons pointing out. Darek's father, Clep, and several other men aimed up at the Great Blue.

"Father, no!" Darek shrieked. He ran out beneath the Great Blue's legs and waved his arms.

"Darek!" yelled his father. "Are you all right?"

"I'm fine," Darek shouted. He looked up at the Great Blue. "Wait, please!" he yelled to her. "Let me talk to them."

The Blue reared and tossed her head from side to side. Darek turned back to the hunters. "Lower your weapons," he shouted. "You're making her nervous."

No one made any move to obey.

"Move aside, son," Darek's father called firmly.

"You don't understand," Darek insisted. "They're peaceful. They only fight to defend themselves. They're not the same as the dragons in the old days. They don't even eat flesh!"

Darek's words seemed to bounce off his father's stony face. "*Get out of the way, son!*" he repeated.

Darek turned to Clep. "Clep, you've got to make him listen," he begged.

Clep lowered his bow slightly and glanced uneasily at his father. "Maybe he's telling the truth," Darek heard him say. "Maybe we should listen."

"He is a child!" Darek's father yelled. "What does he know of dragons? Raise your bow!"

Clep raised his bow again, but when he looked up at Darek he seemed torn.

"Please!" Darek shouted again. "I *do* speak the truth." No one but Clep paid him any heed. Even Yoran's father, Bodak, turned a deaf ear to his pleas.

"*Grrrawk! Grrrawk!*" The Great Blue reared back. Flames shot out of her mouth.

"*For the last time,*" Darek's father yelled, "*get out of the way!*"

Darek stood trembling before his father's icy stare. All his life he had wanted nothing more than to make his father proud. Now he stood defying him. Why? Zantor bumped Darek's arm and whimpered. Darek looked down into the dragonling's gentle face and knew why. If killing without cause was what it took to be a man, he wanted no part of it.

The Great Blue roared and lifted her head. Darek saw his father narrow his eyes and train his bow on the dragon. "*Ready!*" he yelled. "*Aim!*"

Darek put his arms around Zantor and closed his eyes.

9

"*Stop!*"

The scream that split the air was piercing enough to be heard above the dragons.

Darek opened his eyes and stared. There, on the ridge beside the twin rocks, stood his mother. Zilah, Yoran's mother, was with her, and so were most of the other village women.

"Mother!" Darek called out.

Darek's father roared. "Are you mad, woman? Get back, or the dragons will tear you to pieces!"

Darek watched, amazed, as his mother and the other women ignored his father's warning and began the dangerous climb toward the cave. The dragons, too, seemed stunned. Even the Great Blue stopped her roaring and thrashing and stood watching.

Darek glanced anxiously at the dragons as his mother and the others struggled for footings. Should the dragons decide to attack, they would be easy pickings.

"Get back, I tell you!" Darek's father repeated, but the women came on. At last Darek's mother reached the mouth of the cave, and Darek rushed into her arms. She hugged him tight, then looked uneasily up at the Great Blue.

"She won't hurt us," Darek said. "She's only protecting her babies."

Darek's mother nodded. She held up her hands. "I have no weapons," she told the Great Blue. Then she folded her arms around Darek again. "I am a mother, like you."

The Great Blue seemed to understand. She nudged Zantor back into the shadows.

"Take the boy and get out of there," Darek's father yelled, "while you've still got the chance!"

Darek's mother stepped to the ledge.

"It is not the dragons I fear," she shouted. "It is you."

Darek stared at his mother. Never in his life had he seen her speak so to his father. The other men stared too, and Darek's father's face grew as red as a burning ember.

"Perhaps I should leave you with the dragons then?" he shouted.

The other women came up and stood behind Darek's mother.

"You will have to leave us all," she said. "We stand together. No longer will we let our sons be slaughtered for this cruel sport."

An angry murmur passed through the men and Darek's father's eyes burned with rage. "*Sport!*" he shouted. "You call it *sport* to defend our people from their enemies?"

Darek's mother looked around at the great dragons on the cliffs. "If these creatures were truly our enemies," she said, "would I be standing unharmed before you now?"

Some of the men began to glance uncomfortably at one another.

"The old days are gone," Darek's mother went on. "We have suffered enough pain. Look at what you have done to Zilah. And to Marla and Deela and all the others whose sons are gone." Darek's mother pulled Darek close and her voice began to tremble. "Look at what you would have done to me today."

Suddenly there was a cry, and Bodak, Yoran's father, dropped to his knees. He put his hands over his face and his shoulders began to shake. He was weeping, Darek realized. A hard lump formed in his throat. He had never seen a man weep before.

There was a moment of stunned and awkward silence, and then, one by one, the men began to lower their weapons.

10

Darek stood by the entrance to the cave. A few ashes were all that remained of the pile of weapons. The dragons were still cautious, but they had allowed the villagers to return safely to the twin rocks. Darek was sure that friendship would come in time. He turned to Zantor. A great sadness filled his heart.

"You've grown already, little friend," he said. "Soon you *will* be the greatest Great Blue of them all."

Zantor thrummed happily.

"You stay with your new mother now," Darek said, "and maybe we'll see each other again some day." Darek started toward the twin rocks. Zantor scuffled after him.

"No," said Darek firmly. "You have to stay."

Zantor stopped obediently and stood watching until Darek reached the ridge. "*Rrronk?*" he cried out.

Darek looked back and waved, then he turned and hurried forward, blinking back tears. Just as he reached the group there was a flutter and a thump, and then Zantor rushed up from behind and stuffed his head under Darek's shirt. "*Thrrummm, thrrummm, thrrummm,*" he said.

Darek giggled and pushed the dragonling away. "Will you cut that out?" he said.

The villagers laughed.

"Looks like you've adopted yourself a dragon," said Zilah.

Darek's father snorted. "No son of mine is going to play nursemaid to any dragon!"

Darek looked at Zantor. Clearly the dragonling wanted to come home with him, and Darek wanted nothing more. If only he could convince his father.

"Father . . . ?" he began.

His father eyed him suspiciously.

"I was thinking," Darek went on, his stomach fluttering, "the dragons could be our friends. They can light cook fires, they can help plow, they can even take us flying. I flew in the Great Blue's pouch. It was *wonderful!*"

In his growing excitement Darek did not notice his father's eyes growing rounder, and his face growing redder.

"*Enough!*" he boomed. "By the twin moons of Zoriak! What madness will you dream up next?" He whirled and stormed away.

Darek stared after him, his heart as heavy

as stone. His mother put a hand on his shoulder and smiled.

"Change is never easy, my son," she said. "Your father has come a long way today. Give him time."

Zilah and Bodak stood nearby. Darek saw Zilah press Bodak's arm and whisper something into his ear. They murmured together, then Bodak nodded gravely.

"Your words are not easy to accept, young Darek," he said, "but they have much wisdom. Bring the orphan along. Zilah and I will care for him until your father is ready to listen."

Darek's heart leaped with joy, but he bowed his head humbly. "Thank you, Bodak," he said. "You honor me."

"And *I* honor my brother as well."

Darek looked up. Clep was standing before him, holding out the dragonclaw necklace. "This belongs to you," he said.

Darek was confused. "But why?" he asked. "You earned it."

Clep shook his head. "I just got lucky," he said. "It took true courage to do what you did today."

Darek's heart swelled with pride at Clep's praise. He took the prize and held it up. Somehow it brought him no joy now. He heard Zantor whimper beside him. Slowly he lowered his hand again. How could he return the gift to Clep without appearing ungrateful?

Clep seemed to understand. "Perhaps," he said quietly, "it really belongs to the dragons."

Together Darek and Clep dug a hole and buried the necklace between the twin rocks. Then they stood for a moment, side by side, looking out over the valley, peaceful and still now in the late afternoon shadows. Zantor wiggled in between them.

"*Thrummm, thrrummm, thrrummm,*" he said.